An AudioCraft Publishing, Inc. book

Book storage and warehouses provided by Chillermania!©
Indian River, Michigan

Warehouse security provided by:
Lily Munster and Scooby-Boo

Freddie Fernortner, Fearless First Grader
Book 8: Chipper's Crazy Carnival
ISBN 13-digit: 978-1-893699-77-9

Printed in USA

CHIPPER'S
CRAZY
CARNIVAL

VISIT CHILLERMANIA!

WORLD HEADQUARTERS FOR BOOKS BY JOHNATHAN RAND!

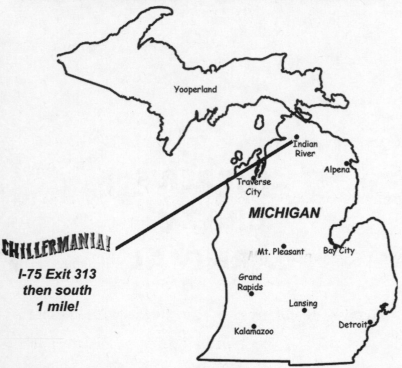

Yooperland

Indian River

Alpena

Traverse City

MICHIGAN

Mt. Pleasant

Bay City

Grand Rapids

Lansing

Detroit

Kalamazoo

CHILLERMANIA!

**I-75 Exit 313
then south
1 mile!**

Visit the HOME for books by Johnathan Rand! Featuring books, hats, shirts, bookmarks and other cool stuff not available anywhere else in the world! Plus, watch the American Chillers website for news of special events and signings at *CHILLERMANIA!* with author Johnathan Rand! Located in northern lower Michigan, on I-75! Take exit 313 . . . then south 1 mile! For more info, call (231) 238-0338. And be afraid! Be veeeery afraaaaaaiiiid . . . .

1

Freddie Fernortner was excited, and he had good reason to be. You see, Freddie and his pals, Chipper and Darla, had come up with a great way to earn some money. Best of all, it would be a lot of fun.

Chipper was the one who had the idea of having a carnival in his backyard. People could play fun games and win prizes. Everyone would have a great time.

Even Mr. Chewy, Freddie's cat, was excited. Mr. Chewy got his name because he liked to chew gum and blow bubbles. He was a good cat, too, and he followed Freddie everywhere he went. Mr. Chewy was the kind of cat any girl or boy would want to have as a friend.

One morning, Freddie woke up and dressed very quickly. This was the day he, Chipper, and Darla would make plans for their carnival.

While Freddie was eating his bowl of cereal, his mother came into the kitchen.

"Guess what?" Freddie said, nearly shouting. He was, after all, very excited.

"What?" his mother asked.

"Chipper, Darla and I are going to have a carnival in Chipper's backyard!" he said as he scooped another spoonful of cereal out of the bowl.

"That sounds fun," his mother said with

a smile.

"It will be!" Freddie said.

"Don't talk with your mouth full," his mother reminded him.

Freddie finished chewing. "We're going to have a blast!" he said. "And we're going to earn money, too!"

"It sounds like it will be a lot of work," his mother said.

Freddie shook his head. "No, it won't!" he replied. "It'll be easy! We're going to make plans and figure everything out today!"

However, plans don't always work out the way you want them to.

Do you think it would be easy for Freddie, Chipper, and Darla to have a carnival in Chipper's backyard?

Maybe.

Do you think everything would go as

planned?

Not hardly!

Freddie, Darla, and Chipper were about to find out that their carnival wasn't going to go as planned at all. In fact, some of the things that would happen were going to be quite scary.

So, if you get scared easily, you might not want to read any more of this story. It might just be better for you to put the book down and find another one.

But if you think you're brave, and you want to find out what happened to Freddie, Chipper, Darla, and Mr. Chewy, then turn the page . . . .

2

After breakfast, Freddie found a piece of paper and a pencil. Then, he and Mr. Chewy went to Chipper's house, where Chipper was waiting for them on the porch. Soon, Darla arrived, and they began to make plans.

"First," Chipper said, "we have to figure out what kind of games to have."

"I know!" Darla said. "We could have a sack race!"

"That's a good idea, Darla," Chipper said. "But we would need to find some sacks to use."

They all thought about it . . . that is, except for Mr. Chewy. He had found a bug on the porch, and he was watching it as it crawled away.

"Hey!" Chipper said. "Why don't we use plastic garbage bags?"

"Good thinking!" Freddie said, and he jotted a few notes on his paper. "What else?" he asked.

"How about a bucket toss?" Chipper said. "Kids could try to toss a tennis ball into a bucket. They'll get three tries, and if they get a ball in the bucket, they'll win a prize."

"Another great idea!" Freddie said, and he wrote it down on his paper.

The three first graders kept thinking. Mr.

Chewy chewed his gum, blew a bubble, and continued watching the bug on the porch.

"How about a game where kids try to knock over plastic bottles with tennis balls?" Freddie asked.

"That would be fun!" Darla said.

"Yeah!" Chipper agreed. "Write that down!"

Freddie wrote it down.

"Hey," Darla said, "do you remember the game we played at my birthday party?"

"Pin the tail on the donkey!" Freddie said. "That's another good one!"

And he wrote it down.

"How about a rubber duckie game?" Chipper said.

"What's that?" Darla asked.

"Well, we can fill a wading pool with water," Chipper said, "and put in a bunch of rubber duckies. One rubber duckie will have the word 'winner' on the bottom. Kids get three tries to pick that rubber duckie. If they do, they win a prize!"

Darla's eyes lit up. "That will be fun!" she said.

"But rubber duckies might cost a lot of money," Freddie said. "Let's use blocks of wood instead."

"Perfect!" Darla said.

So Freddie wrote down that idea, too. "That's five games," he said, looking at his paper. "That will be enough."

"Everyone is going to have a lot of fun!" Chipper exclaimed.

"Yeah," said Freddie, "including us. Let's get started."

"I'll see if my mom will let us have some plastic garbage bags," said Chipper.

"I'll find my pin the tail on the donkey game," said Darla.

"I'll find some blocks of wood," Freddie said. "Let's meet back here in a little while."

The three friends went their separate ways, each with their own job to do. Freddie found a bunch of small wood blocks in his garage, and he placed them in his wagon and took them to Chipper's.

But when he got there, Darla and Chipper looked sad.

"What's the matter?" Freddie asked.

"We forgot one important thing," Darla said. "We have a big problem."

3

Darla explained what was wrong.

"We don't have any prizes," she said. "What are we going to give the winners?"

That *was* a problem. After all, who would pay money to play games if there were no prizes?

So, the three first graders sat on the porch and thought about it. Even Mr. Chewy looked deep in thought.

"Well," Freddie said, "we could buy some prizes at the dollar store."

"That would work!" Chipper said. "We could each chip in a little money that we earned from our dog walking service!"

The three first graders thought it was a good idea. You see, not long ago, they earned money by walking dogs in their neighborhood. And they had a lot of fun, too.

"We could buy stuffed animals," Darla said. "Everybody loves to win stuffed animals."

"Perfect!" Chipper said.

"This is going to be cool!" Freddie said.

After lunch, Freddie's mom drove them to the dollar store, where they bought lots of small stuffed animals. They bought stuffed kitties, puppies, bunnies, monkeys, elephants, penguins, and horses.

And they were very excited. The three first graders knew their carnival was going to be a lot of fun for everyone. On their way home, they chatted in the back seat of the car.

"We've got some great games for kids to play!" Darla said.

"And cool prizes for kids to win!" Freddie said.

Suddenly, Chipper's mouth dropped open, and he looked very worried. "Uh-oh," he said. "We've got another problem!"

Why was Chipper so worried? Turn the page to find out!

4

"How are we going to let kids know about our carnival?" Chipper asked. "If no one knows about it, no one will show up."

Freddie and Darla thought hard.

"Hmm," said Freddie. "I wonder what we could do?"

"I know!" Darla said. "We could put it on television!"

"That would work," Freddie said, "but I

think it would cost more money than we have."

"Maybe we could make posters and put them on telephone poles and trees," Darla said.

Freddie snapped his fingers. "That's a great idea, Darla!" he said. "We can make our own posters with paper and crayons! All we have to do is pick a day to have our carnival!"

"How about Saturday?" Chipper said.

"That would be good," Darla said. "Saturday is my favorite day of the week."

"Let's make our posters!" Freddie said. "Then, we'll post them up around the block to let everyone know about our carnival!"

Freddie, Chipper, and Darla each went home to make posters. Even Mr. Chewy helped out by picking up crayons with his mouth and handing them to Freddie.

Later that day, the three friends went around the neighborhood and tacked their posters on telephone poles. When they saw other friends in the neighborhood, they told them all about the carnival on Saturday.

"What's next?" Darla asked as the three first graders sat on the porch at Chipper's house.

"Let's get our games together and make sure they work," Freddie said.

"That'll be fun!" Chipper said. "We can play our own games for free!"

And so, for the rest of the day, that's what they did. They practiced pinning the tail on the donkey. They played the bucket toss game and the bottle knock-down game. They even filled a small wading pool to practice the rubber duck game. Of course, they didn't have any rubber ducks, but Darla painted the word 'winner' on one of the blocks and placed it upside down in the water. The game worked great.

Chipper's mother wouldn't let him use plastic garbage bags for the sack race. Instead, she gave him a few old pillowcases to use.

"We're ready for our big carnival!" Chipper said. "I can't wait!"

"Neither can I!" Freddie said.

"Uh-oh," Darla said. A worried look came over her face. "We have another problem."

Darla was right. The three first graders had once again forgotten something very important . . . .

5

"Think about it," Darla said. "We have five games."

"Five *great* games!" Chipper said.

"Yes," Darla agreed. "But there are only *three* of us. We need to find some helpers. If lots of kids come to our carnival, we're going to need some help."

Chipper scratched his head. "Yeah, good thinking," he said. "Boy . . . having a carnival is a lot more work than I thought."

"Maybe we can get some of our neighborhood friends to help out," Freddie said.

"That's a great idea, Freddie," Darla said. "We could even pay them! I'll bet we could find some friends who would want to earn money!"

"And they would probably like working at the carnival, too!" Chipper said.

The three first graders and Mr. Chewy got busy. They went all around the neighborhood, talking to friends, asking if they'd like to work at their carnival. Soon, they had three kids who agreed to help out . . . and they were finally ready for the big day.

"I can't wait until tomorrow!" Chipper said. "This is going to be the best carnival in the world!"

"We're going to have a lot of fun!" Darla said.

"I bet a lot of people will come," said Freddie.

Still, there was one thing the three first graders hadn't counted on.

In fact, it was a problem so big, they might not be able to have the carnival!

6

It was the big day.

Saturday.

But Freddie didn't awake to the sound of birds singing in the trees. He didn't awake to warm sunshine streaming through his bedroom window.

In fact, when he awoke, the sky was very, very dark and filled with large, puffy storm clouds.

Freddie climbed out of bed and walked to the window. Mr. Chewy had been sleeping at the bottom of Freddie's bed, and he woke up. He bounced to the floor, then leapt onto Freddie's dresser. Both looked up into the dark sky.

"Uh-oh, Mr. Chewy," Freddie said as he scratched his cat's back. "It looks like a storm is coming."

And he realized if it rained, they might not be able to open their carnival. After all, no one would want to play games in the rain!

Freddie dressed and ate his breakfast quickly. Then, he raced down the street to Chipper's house. Mr. Chewy scampered after him, but he had a hard time keeping up because Freddie was running so fast.

Chipper was sitting on the street curb, looking up into the dark sky. He looked sad.

"If it rains, we can't have our carnival," he said glumly.

Freddie sat down next to him, and Mr. Chewy sat in the grass. All three stared into the sky.

Soon, Darla arrived. She, too, looked sad as she sat on the curb next to Freddie and Chipper.

"I guess we didn't think about the weather," she said.

"I was hoping it would be sunny and warm," Freddie said.

The three first graders waited.

Mr. Chewy chewed his gum and blew bubbles.

After a few minutes, Freddie pointed at the sky.

"Look," he said.

"What is it?" Darla asked.

"There's some blue sky, right there!" Freddie replied.

And there was. The dark storm clouds were slowly breaking up, and little patches of blue sky were appearing.

"The storm clouds are going away!" Chipper said.

While they watched, more and more blue sky appeared. Every once in a while, the sun peeked through the clouds.

"Hurray!" Chipper shouted as he rose to his feet. "We can have our carnival!"

The three first graders raced to Chipper's backyard and went to work. They set up tables and prepared the games. They made everything ready.

Their helpers arrived, and they went to work, too. While they worked, other kids began to arrive and gaze over the fence.

"Look!" Freddie said, pointing to the growing crowd by the backyard gate. "We have customers!"

"We'll be opening soon!" Chipper shouted to the waiting group of children. "Everyone will have a lot of fun!"

After the games and tables were set up, the three first graders went into Chipper's house, where his mother had prepared some snacks and lemonade. They carried the food and the pitchers and cups outside and placed them on one of the tables. They were sure some of their customers would get hungry.

Finally, when the carnival was ready, it was time to open the gate. Chipper's carnival was about to open for business!

Freddie thought everything was going to be perfect. So did Chipper and Darla.

But do *you* think everything was going to

be perfect?

If you said 'no,' you're right . . . because their backyard carnival was about to go haywire!

7

Chipper looked around the backyard where all the tables were set. He looked at the games to make sure everything was in order.

"Everybody ready?" he shouted.

"You bet!" Freddie shouted.

"Me, too!" Darla said.

The three helpers were ready, too.

Chipper turned to the group of waiting children. "Are you ready?" he asked.

The group cheered and clapped.

Then, Chipper walked to the gate and opened it. "Come in!" he said with a sweep of his arm. "Enjoy our carnival!"

The children cheered again, and the group poured through the gate. Soon, kids were playing the bucket toss game. They had fun trying to knock over plastic bottles with a tennis ball. Others were playing pin the tail on the donkey and the sack race. Everyone was smiling and happy.

And more and more children came.

They played the rubber duckie game. Which, of course, wasn't a rubber duckie game at all . . . but the children playing the game didn't mind. They laughed as they plucked blocks of wood from the wading pool, hoping to get the one with the word 'winner' on the bottom. Everyone was having a grand time.

Still, more and more children came. Mr. Chewy was having a difficult time moving about, because there were so many children that they didn't even see him! He had to be very careful so he didn't get stepped on.

Soon, there were so many kids in Chipper's backyard that nobody could move . . . and that's when disaster struck.

8

Chipper's carnival was a huge success, and that was the problem. There were too many children in the backyard!

Suddenly, someone bumped the snack table, and it tipped over. Cookies and candy tumbled into the grass.

Then, the table with the pitchers of lemonade tipped over, and everyone standing nearby was soaked with the sweet, sticky liquid!

And if that wasn't bad enough, a little girl was accidentally bumped, and she fell into the rubber duck game! She stood up quickly, soaking wet from head to toe!

Freddie made his way through the crowd of kids until he reached the girl.

"Are you okay?" he asked.

The girl nodded. "I'm fine, but I'm all wet," she said.

"I'm covered in lemonade!" a boy said angrily.

"Me too!" said a little girl.

"I'm really sorry," Freddie said.

Chipper pushed through the crowd and made his way to Freddie, followed by Darla.

"There are too many people in the yard," Chipper said. "We'll have to ask some people to leave."

41

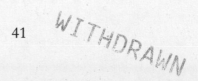

"Maybe if we ask them nicely, they'll wait," Darla said.

Freddie cupped his hands around his mouth.

"Hey, everyone!" he shouted. "We need your help! We need everyone to leave the backyard and form a line! If you can do that, we can start letting small groups of people start playing games again!"

Chipper cupped his hands around his mouth. "And it won't be so crowded!" he shouted.

Darla cupped her hands around her mouth. "Please?" she shouted.

Slowly, all of the children began filing out through the fence. Then, they formed a line, just like Freddie asked. The girl that fell into the wading pool went home to get into dry clothing. So did the boy and girl that had been splashed with lemonade.

"It will be just a minute, everyone!" Freddie shouted. "We have to clean things up!"

The three first graders and their three helpers got busy. They righted the tables that had been knocked over. They picked up all the spilled snacks and put them in the garbage can. Chipper ran inside with the empty lemonade pitchers and returned a few minutes later. His mother had made more lemonade, and he carefully placed the pitchers on the table. All the while, Mr. Chewy sat near a tree, chewing gum and blowing bubbles, watching the three first graders work.

"Let's not make that mistake again," Freddie said.

"We won't," Chipper said. "Come on. Let's let our customers back in!"

Freddie walked over to the fence. "Okay, everyone!" he called out. "We're ready to go again, but everyone will have to wait to take their turn! We'll let ten people in at a time. When they're done playing games, we'll let them out. Then, we'll let in ten more. Is that okay?"

The kids cheered and clapped. They didn't mind waiting, because the carnival games were so much fun.

And the plan worked perfectly. The children played the games and had fun. When they were done, they carried away their stuffed animal prizes, and ten more kids were allowed in. Everyone was having a great time . . . until some big kids arrived.

And they weren't going to be very nice.

9

At first, no one noticed the three big kids that rode up on their bicycles. They stopped near the backyard fence and watched as the younger children played games and had fun. One of the big kids was wearing a baseball cap.

Without warning, the three big kids pushed their way through the gate and into the backyard.

Chipper saw them. "I'm sorry," he told the three big kids. "You'll have to wait your turn."

"I'm not waiting for anything," the big kid with the baseball hat said. He crossed his arms. "I want to play a game, and I want to play it *now*."

"Yeah, me, too," another big kid said.

Freddie walked over to the three big kids. "You'll have to wait your turn or leave," he said.

"Oh, yeah?" the big kid with the baseball hat said. He reached out and poked Freddie's chest with his finger. "Who's going to make us?"

Freddie was beginning to get scared, and so were Chipper and Darla. After all, the three big kids were older and bigger than the three first graders.

Some of the children playing games were watching the three big kids. They stopped playing and walked over to where Freddie and Chipper were standing. Soon, all of the kids in the carnival had surrounded the three big kids.

"We don't want any bullies spoiling our fun," someone said. "If you don't leave, we're going to tell Chipper's mom and dad."

"Yeah," another kid said. "You should go home. Stop trying to spoil our fun."

Even the children waiting on the other side of the fence were angry.

"Yeah, you'd better leave," a girl said, "or else you're going to be in big trouble."

The three big kids looked around. Although they were bigger than all the other children, they were outnumbered.

"Come on, guys," the big kid with the baseball hat said. "Let's get out of here. I don't want to play any boring carnival games, anyway."

And so, the three big kids left the backyard, hopped on their bikes, and rode off.

"Whew," Chipper said. "I thought those big kids were going to cause a lot of trouble."

Soon, all the kids were playing games again and having a great time.

In fact, everyone was having so much fun that no one even noticed the dark, scary clouds headed their way.

The storm that had broken up earlier in the day was coming back . . . and this time, it wasn't going away.

10

Everyone was having such a good time that no one noticed the sun had gone away. No one noticed that the wind was getting stronger. No one saw the dark clouds looming high above, coming closer and closer.

Suddenly, there was a rumble of thunder. It was so loud that the ground trembled, and everyone stopped playing games and looked up into the sky. Even Mr. Chewy, who had been sitting by a tree, looked up.

"Uh-oh," Darla said as she stared at the darkening sky. "It looks like it might rain."

As soon as she said those words, a big raindrop fell on her forehead. Another landed on her cheek. And another. The wind began to blow, bending the trees and tearing leaves from their branches.

All at once, the sky opened up, pouring buckets and buckets of rain on the children. Everyone ran out the gate, heading for cover. Freddie, Chipper, Darla, Mr. Chewy, and the three helpers ran to the front of Chipper's house and ducked into the garage, but it was too late. They were already soaked from head to toe.

"What a bummer!" Chipper said glumly.

"So much for our carnival," Darla said.

The three first graders and their three

helpers could only watch as the rain poured down. Puddles formed in the street and in the driveway. Thunder rumbled, and a bolt of lightning flashed. Mr. Chewy got scared and leapt into Freddie's arms.

"But," Freddie said, "it's a good thing we're inside the garage. I wouldn't want to be outside with all that lightning."

All they could do was wait.

And wait.

And wait even more.

But soon, an amazing thing happened.

11

The three first graders and their three helpers, along with Mr. Chewy, were in the garage watching the rain fall.

Suddenly, Darla pointed to the sky.

"Look!" she shouted. "Look at that!"

Everyone, including Mr. Chewy, looked to see where Darla was pointing.

"Wow!" Chipper gasped. "That's cool!"

High in the sky, a long way off, a

rainbow was forming. It had all kinds of beautiful colors.

"That's the first rainbow I've ever seen!" Freddie said.

The children were amazed, and they continued gazing at the colorful rainbow in the sky.

Soon, the rain went away. Clouds began to break up, and the sun came out again, shining on the wet grass and trees and rooftops.

"Hurray!" the children shouted. They clapped their hands. Even Mr. Chewy put his paws together, but, when he did, they didn't make any noise. Still, he was just as excited as the three first graders and their helpers.

"Let's get into dry clothing and open the carnival again!" Chipper said.   And that's what they did. They all raced to their homes to change into dry clothing. Soon, the three first graders and their three helpers were all gathered in Chipper's backyard again. They got to work wiping the rain off the tables and picking up the snacks, which were now soggy and ruined.

"At least the rain didn't hurt any of our games," Freddie said.

"Yeah," Chipper said, "a little water didn't hurt anything. We'll be back in business in no time!"

Very soon, they were ready. Now, however, they had another big problem . . . .

12

"Chipper," Darla said, "everyone went home. Nobody knows that our carnival is open again. We don't have any customers."

The first graders all agreed: it was a big problem.

"What can we do to let everyone know our carnival is open again?" Chipper said.

The three first graders thought about it. Their helpers thought about it. Even Mr.

Chewy thought about it.

Finally, Freddie snapped his fingers. "I've got it!" he cried. "Chipper, let's make a bullhorn!"

Chipper looked puzzled. "What's a bullhorn?" he asked.

"It's a horn we can make out of paper or cardboard," Freddie replied. "It looks a lot like a giant ice cream cone."

"But Freddie," Darla said, "what good is a horn going to do?"

"Well," Freddie said, "it's not really a horn. You put one end of it to your mouth and shout into it. The bullhorn makes your voice really loud. We can use it to tell everyone that our carnival is open again. But first, we'll need a big piece of cardboard."

"I think there's some cardboard in our garage," Chipper said. "I'll be right back."

Chipper raced to the front of his house and returned a few minutes later with a big, thin piece of cardboard. He handed it to Freddie.

"Watch," Freddie said as he carefully rolled the cardboard. While he worked, he made sure one end was small, and the other end was very large. Soon, the cardboard square had taken on a new shape. Now, it looked like a large ice cream cone, just like Freddie had said it would.

"Now," said Freddie, "all we have to do is go around the neighborhood. I'll use my bullhorn to let everyone know that our carnival is open again!"

"I have an idea," Chipper said. He pointed to Freddie's wagon that sat near the fence. Freddie had used it to haul the wood blocks from his house. "Let's tie your wagon to my bike," Chipper continued. "I can pedal around the block, and you and Darla and Mr. Chewy can ride in the wagon. That way, we can go faster!"

Darla spoke. "The faster we let everyone know that our carnival is open, the faster they will come back!" she said.

"Great idea!" Freddie exclaimed. He turned to their helpers. "You guys stay here and wait for customers," he said. "We'll be back soon!"

Chipper raced to his garage to get his bike and a rope, while Freddie and Darla ran to their homes to get their bike helmets. By the time they returned, Chipper had already tied the wagon to his bike.

"Ready?" Darla asked.

"Let's go!" Chipper said.

Freddie and Darla leapt into the wagon.

"Come on, Mr. Chewy!" Freddie shouted. "There's room for you, too!"

Mr. Chewy scampered to the wagon and leapt up, taking a seat in the back.

"Ready to go, Chipper!" Freddie said, holding the bullhorn with both hands. "Pedal around the block on the sidewalk, and I'll start letting everyone know our carnival is open again!"

And, as you can imagine, things weren't going to go as planned for the three first graders and Mr. Chewy. They didn't know it yet, but something *awful* was about to happen.

Hang on tight . . . Freddie, Darla, and Mr. Chewy are in for the ride of their lives!

13

Chipper started pedaling, and the wagon began rolling on the sidewalk.

"This will be great!" Chipper shouted. "We'll be able to go all around the block and let everyone know that the rain didn't spoil our carnival!"

As the bike and wagon went faster, Freddie held the bullhorn up to his lips. "HEY EVERYONE!" he shouted. "THE

CARNIVAL AT CHIPPER'S HOUSE IS OPEN! COME ON OVER AND HAVE A GREAT TIME!"

And because he was using his homemade bullhorn, his voice carried much farther. Kids in their houses heard his message and came outdoors.

"Your carnival is open again?" someone shouted from his front porch.

"YES!" Freddie shouted back. "COME OVER TO CHIPPER'S AND PLAY OUR SUPER-FUN GAMES!"

As the wagon bounced along the sidewalk and around the block, Freddie kept shouting into his bullhorn, letting everyone know that the carnival was open once again. But as they rounded the corner to turn onto another street, the bike and the wagon hit a bump. Normally, this wouldn't have caused a problem. However, what they didn't know was that the wagon handle was loose. When the wagon hit the bump, it was all that was needed to make the handle fall off! It hit the sidewalk with a loud *clunk,* and the wagon was no longer hooked to Chipper's bicycle!

What could be worse?

Well, the street they were on was at the top of the hill, and now Freddie, Darla, and Mr. Chewy were speeding down it, out of control, with no way to steer and no way to stop!

Oh, no!

14

Very quickly, Freddie and Darla realized they were in a lot of trouble.

"Chipper!" Freddie shouted. "Help! Help us!"

Chipper glanced over his shoulder and saw Freddie, Darla, and Mr. Chewy in the wagon. The handle was still tied to the rope, but it was no longer connected to the wagon, which was going faster and faster as it raced down the hill, out of control.

"Freddie!" Darla shouted. "Freddie, do something!"

"I can't steer!" Freddie shouted. "And this thing doesn't have any brakes!"

Mr. Chewy was terrified, and he put his paws over his eyes. Darla was terrified, and she covered her eyes with her hands. Freddie was scared, too, but he didn't cover his eyes. He was too busy thinking about how he was going to stop the out-of-control wagon!

All the while, they were moving faster and faster and faster, until they had finally caught up with Chipper.

"How do we stop this thing?!?!" Freddie shouted.

"I don't know!" Chipper shouted back. "It's never happened before!"

And the wagon kept going faster and

faster. In fact, it was going so fast, Chipper was having a hard time keeping up with it!

"Jump out!" Chipper screamed as he pedaled as fast as he could.

"We're going too fast!" Freddie shouted.

All of a sudden, the wagon hit a bump, throwing it off the sidewalk and into a yard. The wagon bounced through the grass, heading straight for a tree!

15

CRASH!

The wagon hit the tree, sending Freddie, Darla, and Mr. Chewy flying into the air. In fact, they hit the trunk so hard that it flung them up into the tree, where they all became stuck in the branches!

Chipper stopped and leapt off his bike.

"Freddie!" he shouted. "Darla! Are you okay?!?!"

For a moment, no one said anything, and Chipper thought his friends were hurt.

Finally, Freddie spoke.

"I'm okay," he said. "Are you all right, Darla?"

"I'm fine," Darla said. "But I think I'm stuck."

Mr. Chewy dropped to the ground, landing on all four paws. He sat in the grass and looked up at the two first graders in the tree.

After some squirming and wiggling, Freddie was able to free himself from the tangle of branches. He dropped out of the tree and landed on his feet. Darla, too, wiggled free and dropped safely to the ground.

"You guys were really lucky!" Chipper said. "You could have been hurt!"

"It's a good thing we had our helmets

on," Freddie said. "Are you all right, Mr. Chewy?"

Mr. Chewy, of course, didn't say a word, because everyone knows cats can't talk. Instead, he blew a bubble and flipped his tail around.

"Well, I hope everyone knows that our carnival is open again," Darla said.

"Yeah," Freddie said. "Let's head back to your house, Chipper."

"First," said Chipper, "we have to try and fix your wagon. Let's see if we can put the handle back on."

It took a few minutes, but the three first graders were able to connect the handle to the wagon.

"There," Chipper said. "All fixed."

"Let's not pull it behind your bike this time," Darla said.

"Yeah," Freddie said. "We'll just pull it behind us. Hop in the wagon, Mr. Chewy, and you can go for a ride."

The cat scampered to the wagon and leapt inside. Freddie picked up the handle and pulled the wagon, and Darla walked alongside.

Chipper pushed his bike as he walked. "Having a carnival sure is a lot of work," he said.

Darla nodded. "It sure is," she said.

"Yeah," Freddie agreed. "But it sure is a lot of fun. I hope all of our customers come back."

"They will," Chipper said. "Now that the rain has gone away and the sun is out, everyone will want to play our games again."

The three first graders continued walking and were almost to Chipper's house when Darla suddenly stopped.

Then, Freddie stopped.

Chipper stopped, too.

The three first graders said nothing. They could only stare.

There was a police car in front of Chipper's house!

16

"Uh-oh," Freddie said.

"Do you think we did something wrong?" Darla asked.

Chipper shook his head. "I don't think so," he said. "But maybe it's against the law to have a carnival in my backyard."

"What if we go to jail?" Darla said. Her voice trembled with fear.

"I don't think we can get into trouble for

having a carnival," Freddie said. "There must be something else wrong. Come on. Let's go find out what it is."

The three first graders and Mr. Chewy started walking again. They stopped when they reached the police car. Mr. Chewy sat on the sidewalk next to Freddie, chewing his gum and blowing bubbles.

"There's no policeman in the police car," Freddie said as he peered through the window.

Darla pointed down the street. "It's not a police *man*," she said. "It's a police *woman*. And there she is, over there!"

They all turned to see the police woman walking toward them. She was carrying something small and white in her arms. When she saw the three first graders, she smiled and waved.

"She doesn't look like she's mad at us,"

Chipper said.

"What's she carrying in her arms?" Darla asked.

"It looks like a small, white pillow," said Freddie.

They continued watching as the police woman walked toward them.

"It looks like she's carrying a dog," Chipper said.

"It is a dog," said Darla. "It's a little white poodle."

"Hello," the police woman said with a wave of her hand.

"Hi," Freddie said. "What's your dog's name?"

The police woman laughed. "This is Pixie," she said, "but she's not my dog. She belongs to Mrs. Davis on the next block. Pixie dug a hole under the fence and ran away. Mrs.

Davis has been worried sick all day."

"She's going to be happy when she finds out her dog is safe," Darla said.

"Yes, she will," the police woman said as she reached the car. "I'm happy, too. I've been trying to catch Pixie for fifteen minutes."

At that moment, Pixie let out a bark.

And a growl.

She'd spotted Mr. Chewy . . . and leapt from the arms of the police woman!

Mr. Chewy ran off, with Pixie right behind him.

The chase was on!

17

Pixie the little white poodle darted past the three first graders. Mr. Chewy scampered across the grass and headed for the nearest tree.

"Hurry, Mr. Chewy!" Freddie cried.

"Stop, Pixie, stop!" shouted the police woman.

But the little poodle wasn't listening. The dog was too busy trying to catch Freddie's cat.

Mr. Chewy made it to the tree and climbed up the trunk. He stopped when he reached a branch and then looked down. Below, Pixie the white poodle was yapping and barking and running around the tree trunk.

The three first graders and the police woman raced to the tree.

"Don't move, Mr. Chewy!" Freddie shouted to his cat. "We'll save you!"

Pixie the poodle continued barking. She ran circles around the tree trunk. All the while, she kept looking up at Mr. Chewy, perched on a branch.

The police woman moved quickly. She reached down and picked up the dog with both hands, then cradled her in her arms.

"You sure are causing all sorts of trouble today," she said to the little dog. "I'm going to put you in the car and take you back to Mrs.

Davis before you cause any more problems."

Then, the police woman looked at Mr. Chewy sitting on the tree branch. "Do you need help getting your cat down?" she asked Freddie.

"No," Freddie said. "He'll climb down, just as soon as that poodle is gone."

"Well, you children have a good day. I don't think Pixie will be stirring up any more trouble."

As soon as the police woman got in her car with the poodle, Mr. Chewy scampered down the tree.

"Don't worry, buddy," Freddie said to his cat. He patted Mr. Chewy's head. "That doggie is all gone."

"He was lucky," Darla said. "That poodle was—"

Suddenly, Chipper gasped, causing Darla

to stop speaking. He pointed.

"Oh, my gosh!" he shouted. "Look!"

And when Freddie and Darla saw what Chipper was pointing at, they, too, gasped in amazement.

18

Near Chipper's backyard, a crowd had gathered again. They were lined up, waiting to get into the carnival! Their three helpers were waiting by the gate, too.

"Come on!" Chipper shouted. "We've got work to do!"

The three first graders ran to the side of Chipper's house and into the backyard. When the crowd of children saw them, they cheered.

"Your idea worked, Freddie," Darla said as they made their way to the gate. "That bullhorn you made worked great!"

"Are we ready to open?" Freddie asked.

"Yep!" Chipper replied. Then, he shouted to the crowd of waiting kids. "Are you guys ready to have fun?"

The kids cheered.

"Let's get busy!" Darla said. Chipper opened the gate, and he counted as ten kids filed through. Then, he closed the gate.

"As soon as they're done," Chipper told the crowd, "we'll let ten more people in."

For the rest of the day, people played games in Chipper's backyard. Everyone had a lot of fun, including the helpers. Despite all the trouble they'd had, Chipper's carnival was a big success.

Later, when everyone had gone home

and they'd put all the games away and cleaned up the yard, the three first graders sat on Chipper's porch, sipping lemonade. Darla was busy counting all the money they'd earned. Mr. Chewy sat with them, blowing bubbles.

"After we paid our helpers, we have twenty-one dollars and seventy-five cents!" Darla said as she finished counting the money.

Freddie found a piece of paper and a pencil and went to work. After a moment, he spoke. "That means we each get to keep seven dollars and twenty-five cents!"

"We're rich!" Darla said as she counted the money again. She gave Chipper and Freddie their share.

"What a fun day," Chipper said as he stuffed his money in his pocket. "We'll have to do that again."

"Yeah," said Darla. "We should have a

carnival every summer!"

When they finished their lemonade, they said good-bye to one another. Freddie and Mr. Chewy walked home. When they arrived, Mrs. Fernortner was just putting dinner on the table.

"I was just about to call for you," she said. "Get cleaned up and take your place at the table."

During dinner, Freddie told his mom and dad all about their carnival. He showed them the money he'd earned. His parents were very proud of him.

Afterwards, he helped his mother with the dirty dishes. Later, they watched a movie on television and had popcorn.

Finally, it was time for Freddie to go to bed. He fell asleep quickly. After all, it had been a long day, and he was very tired.

But he was happy.

In the morning, he awoke to the delicious smell of chocolate chip cookies.

Cookies for breakfast? he thought as he climbed out of bed. He walked into the kitchen where his mother was busy putting a tray into the oven.

"Good morning," Mrs. Fernortner said, and she gave Freddie a kiss and a hug. "How about some breakfast?"

"Yeah," Freddie said. "I love chocolate chip cookies."

His mother smiled and shook her head. "Not for breakfast, you don't," she said. "I'm making these for Mr. and Mrs. Beaker, across the street. I'm going to take the cookies over to them in a little while, and there's something I'd like you to do while I'm gone."

"What?" Freddie asked.

"I'd like you to pick up your room," she said. "You keep it very nice, but it's time to give it a good cleaning, from top to bottom. And that includes under the bed. Okay?"

Freddie nodded. "Okay," he said. It wouldn't take him very long to clean his room.

Or, that's what he *thought*.

Today, however, was going to be different. Today, something was waiting for Freddie under the bed.

Dust bunnies.

Now, you might think that dust bunnies wouldn't cause any trouble. But these weren't ordinary dust bunnies; they were dust bunnies from outer space. They were waiting for Freddie . . . and they were about to attack!

NEXT:
FREDDIE FERNORTNER,
FEARLESS FIRST GRADER

BOOK NINE:

ATTACK OF THE
DUST BUNNIES
FROM
OUTER SPACE!

CONTINUE ON
TO READ
THE FIRST CHAPTER
FOR FREE!

1

Freddie Fernortner, Fearless First Grader, was cleaning his bedroom when he heard a knock on the door. He stopped what he was doing and quickly peered out his window.

On the porch were his two of best friends in the whole world: Darla and Chipper.

Oh, Freddie had another best friend, too. But he was a four-legged, furry friend—a cat, as a matter of fact—named Mr. Chewy.

Mr. Chewy could chew gum and even blow bubbles . . . and that's how he got his name.

And that's what Mr. Chewy was doing when Darla and Chipper knocked. He was sitting on Freddie's bed, chewing gum and blowing bubbles.

Freddie spun, ran out his bedroom, down the hall, and across the living room. He opened the front door.

"Hi, guys!" he said. He was happy to see his friends.

"Hi, Freddie!" Chipper said.

"Chipper and I wanted to know if you want to go to the pond," Darla said.

"Yeah!" Chipper said. His eyes grew wide. "There's a weird creature living in it!"

"In the pond?!?!" Freddie asked.

Darla nodded. "My brother told me all about it. He says the creature hides in the pond, and that it's big and ugly. We're going to go try to find it. Want to come?"

"Man, that sounds like fun," Freddie said. "But my mom is across the street at Mr. and Mrs. Beaker's. She made them some cookies this morning, and asked me to clean my room while she's gone."

"Rats," Darla said.

Suddenly, Chipper had an idea.

"Hey!" he said. "What if Darla and I help you? We could get your room cleaned a lot faster. By the time your mom comes home, we'll be done. Then, we can all go to the pond!"

"And find the creature!" Darla said.

"That *is* a good idea!" Freddie said. "Come on in!"

Chipper and Darla followed Freddie to his bedroom.

"Where do we start?" Chipper asked.

"We need a broom," Freddie said. "Mom wants me to clean under my bed."

Freddie turned and went into the hall. Darla and Chipper followed, until they reached a closet.

"There's a broom in here," Freddie said as he opened the closet door. "And there are some rags and window cleaner on the shelves."

"With our help," Chipper said, "you'll get done a lot faster."

The broom was behind the vacuum cleaner, so Freddie had to reach around to pull it out.

"I'll work on cleaning your bedroom window," Darla said as she plucked the bottle of glass cleaner from the closet shelf.

"And I'll clean off your dresser,"

Chipper said.

The trio walked back to Freddie's bedroom. Mr. Chewy sat quietly on the bed, watching. His tail swished back and forth.

And the three first graders got to work. Darla carefully cleaned the window, and Chipper wiped down the dresser.

"I haven't cleaned beneath my bed in months," Freddie said. "I don't even know what's under it."

He knelt down and swept the broom under the bed . . . but when he did, it was suddenly yanked out of his hands!

The broom vanished beneath the bed!

DON'T MISS FREDDIE FERNORTNER, FEARLESS FIRST GRADER BOOK 9: ATTACK OF THE DUST BUNNIES FROM OUTER SPACE!

WATCH FOR MORE
FREDDIE FERNORTNER, FEARLESS FIRST GRADER BOOKS, COMING SOON!